Written by Laurence Anholt
Illustrated by Arthur Robins

ORCHARD BOOKS
Carmelite House, 50 Victoria Embankment,
London, EC4Y 0DZ
Orchard Books Australia
Hachette Children's Books
Level 17/207 Kent Street, Sydney, NSW 2000

First published in Great Britain in 1996
This edition published in 2016

Text © Laurence Anholt 1996
Illustration © Arthur Robbins 1996

The rights of Laurance Anholt to be identified as the author
and Arthur Robbins as the illustrator of this work
has been asserted by them in accordance with the
Copyright, Designs and Patents Act, 1988.

A CIP catalogue record for this book is available from the British Library

ISBN 978 1 84121 404 7

16

Printed in Great Britain by Clays Ltd, St. Ives plc

☆ The Fried Piper ☆ Shampoozel ☆ Daft Jack ☆ The Emperor ☆
☆ Little Red Riding Wolf ☆ Rumply Crumply Stinky Pin ☆

☆ Ghostyshocks ☆ Snow White ☆ Cinderboy ☆ Eco-Wolf ☆
☆ The Greedy Farmer ☆ Billy Beast ☆

Cinderboy was crazy about football.

His wicked stepdad and his two lazy stepbrothers were football crazy too. The whole family supported Royal Palace United.

Royal Palace are MA-AGIC
Everyone else is TRA-AGIC !

Every Saturday they would lie about on the sofa with the remote control and watch their favourite team on TV. Royal Palace always played brilliantly in their smart pink shorts and shirts.

But not poor Cinderboy. He wasn't even allowed to watch. He had to wait on his stepbrothers hand and foot, and bring them cups of tea and bowl after bowl of peanuts, which were their favourite snack.

Cinderboy's family was very noisy and bad mannered. When Royal Palace scored they would jump up and down on the sofa and shout for more peanuts to celebrate.

And when the other team scored they would throw their peanuts at the TV, then yell at Cinderboy to pick them up so that they could throw them again.

One day his cruel stepfather said to Cinderboy, "Listen, Cinders, tomorrow is the day of the big Cup Final. I am taking your stepbrothers to the Royal Palace stadium to watch the match. And while we are gone you must clean the whole house from top to bottom."

"Yes," said his stepbrothers, "we want every last peanut picked up from under the sofa."

Poor Cinderboy was very unhappy. He would have loved to see his team play in the Cup Final more than anything else in the world.

The next morning he had to wake up
earlier than ever to prepare peanut butter
sandwiches for his horrible brothers who
only laughed at the tears in Cinder's eyes.

As they drove away, shouting and tooting the horn, Cinderboy lay on the sofa and cried and cried and cried.

Then he had an idea. He would work as hard as anything to clean the house so that he could watch the big Cup Final on TV.

He set to work straight away

. . . scrubbing his
stepbrothers' smelly
football socks

. . . and hoovering up every
last peanut from under the sofa.

When at last the work was done, the house sparkled from top to bottom.

Cinderboy pulled up his little stool, found the remote control and switched on the TV.

The match had just begun. The terraces were packed with cheering Royal Palace fans. Cinderboy even caught a glimpse of his stepfather and brothers sitting in the front row, waving their pink scarves and throwing peanuts at the referee.

Oh, how Cinderboy wished he could go to a real live football match!

What made him feel even sadder was that Royal Palace were not playing well that day. Soon the other side had scored and Cinderboy felt sadder than ever.

ROYAL PALACE UNITED - NIL!

GIANTS TEN!

To make matters worse, just before half-
time a terrible thing happened – the Royal
Palace captain was kicked in the shin and
had to be carried off the field on a stretcher.

When the half-time whistle blew, Royal Palace were ten–nil down and struggling without their best player.

During the advertisements Cinderboy was crying so hard he could hardly see the television.

Suddenly, a pink face appeared on the TV screen before him.

"Don't cry, Cindy," it said.

Cinderboy rubbed his eyes. "There must be something wrong with the television," he thought. The face seemed to be talking to *him!*

"Who . . . who . . . who are you?" he stuttered.

"I am your TV Godmother," said the face on the television. "And guess what, Cindy? You *shall* go to the big Cup Final!"

"But I don't have anything to wear," stammered Cinderboy.

"Don't worry, Cinderboy. Just press button 13 on the remote control," said the TV Godmother.

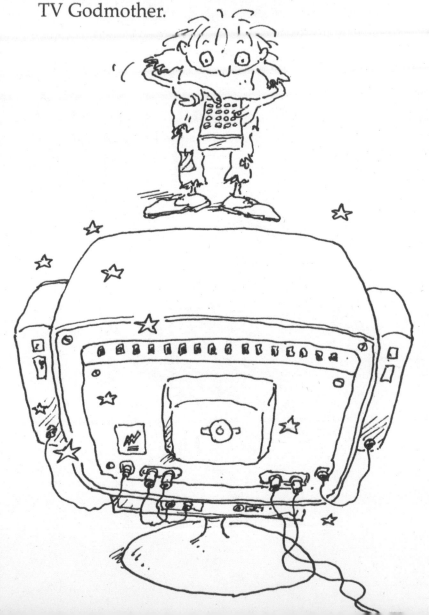

Cinderboy wiped his eyes with the back of his hand and held out the remote control. He pressed button 13.

As if by magic the scruffy old clothes he was wearing disappeared – and Cinderboy stood tall and handsome, dressed in a pink silk shirt and pink silk shorts. On his feet were a pair of brand new football boots with gleaming glass studs.

"Oh, thank you, TV Godmother! But. . . how will I get to the big Cup Final?"

"Oooh, you are a big worrier!" said the voice from the TV. "Press button 14 on the remote control."

Cinderboy pressed button 14.

As if by magic the old sofa changed into a long shiny pink limousine with a pink uniformed chauffeur at the wheel.

"Oh, thank you! Thank you!" cried Cinderboy.

"Just one thing, Cindy doll," said the face on TV, "no one must recognise you. Wear this mask at all times."

A hand reached out of the screen holding a pink silk mask. "And most important of all, you must return home before the referee blows the final whistle."

Without a second thought, Cinderboy grabbed the mask and jumped into the limousine and roared out through the door.

It seemed like only seconds before he screeched to a halt in the stadium car park.

Cinderboy pulled on the pink mask and ran towards a big open door. When he looked around, he was standing . . .

. . . RIGHT IN THE MIDDLE
OF THE PITCH!

The crowd cheered in excitement as the mysterious pink-masked player charged on to the field and headed straight for the ball.

He skilfully tackled the other players, flicking the ball into the air with his left foot and sprinting towards the goal post. Then, to the amazement of the Royal Palace fans – KERBAM! He shot it into the back of the net!

The crowd went wild.

Only ten more minutes to go. Cinderboy manoeuvred the ball around the pitch as gracefully as a dancer at a fairy-tale ball.

Then – KERBOOM! Cinderboy scored again. And – KERBLAM! He headed the ball into the back of the net.

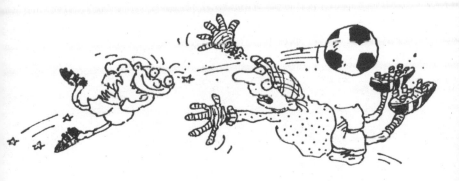

KERWOOMPH! He bounced it into the goal with the tip of his glass-studded boot. The stadium roared with applause.

On a bench at the side of the field the injured Royal Palace captain and Eddy Prince, the team manager, stared in disbelief. "Whoever that player is," they said, "we *need* him for our team."

ROYAL PALACE UNITED

Before long, the score was equal – ten all.
But soon there were only seconds left to
play and the ball was at the wrong end of
the field.

Cinderboy noticed the referee put the whistle to his lips.

"TV Godmother, help me!" he whispered.

One last time Cinderboy dived towards the ball. With a mighty swing he kicked it so hard that one of his glass-studded boots flew off and then tumbled to the ground.

The ball shot upwards like a rocket. The whole crowd rose to their feet.

The rival team stood open-mouthed as the ball soared like a bird through the sky. At the other end of the field it began to fall. It bounced once, then dropped effortlessly into the centre of the net.

Royal Palace had won the Cup Final! The crowd went ballistic! A thousand pink caps were thrown into the air. Eddy Prince raced on to the pitch to sign up the mystery player.

But Cinderboy, remembering the promise
to his TV Godmother, ran out of the stadium
as fast as his one boot would carry him.

But, to his dismay, when he reached
the car park, he found only the battered old
sofa where the pink limousine had been.

And poor old Cinderboy had to push the
sofa home.

The man in the pink mask was fantastic.
Royal Palace were MA·AGIC!
The rest of the world is TRA·AGIC!

"You should have seen him!" shouted the stepbrothers when they finally returned home from the celebrations.

"Yeah!" they smirked, "and poor old Cinderboy missed the whole thing."

Cinderboy only smiled to himself. That night, as he lay in his broken old bed, tears of joy sparkled in his eyes as he dreamed about the day he had scored the winning goal for Royal Palace United, the best team in the whole wide world.

Early the next morning there was a
knock at the door. Cinderboy ran to answer
it. He couldn't believe his eyes! There stood
Eddy Prince, the Royal Palace manager.

"I'm searching for the mysterious boy in the pink mask," he said. "The person who fits this gleaming glass-studded boot will play for the Royal Palace team for the rest of their days."

"Oooh!" said the lazy stepbrothers, coming downstairs in their pyjamas. "Let me try! Let me try! It's no good asking Cinderboy – he didn't even watch the match! Go and fetch some peanuts for Mr Prince, Cinders."

The first greedy stepbrother snatched the glass-studded boot from Eddy Prince.

He tore off his slipper and shoved his sweaty foot into the boot. But no matter how hard he pushed, he couldn't get the boot on.

Then the second greedy stepbrother stepped forward and grabbed the boot.

His foot was slightly smaller and slightly sweatier. He shoved . . .

and squeezed . . .

and pushed . . .

and heaved . . .

and suddenly – PLOP! His foot was inside.

"IT FITS! IT FITS!" he shouted. "Father, Father, come and look! I'm going to play for Royal Palace!

I'm going to be on telly!

I'm going to be rich!

I'm going to buy a peanut factory . . .

Everyone's going to cheer, just like they did for the boy in the pink mask – I mean *me*, of course."

"Oh!" said Eddy Prince, looking a little surprised. "Are you sure it was you? I'm afraid you'll have to do a little training . . ."

Suddenly Cinderboy stepped out of the kitchen.

On his face he wore . . . a pink silk mask!

In his hand was . . . a tiny pair of pink shorts!

"Well then, stepbrother," he said. "Let's see you fit into *these* . . ." And he held out the pink shorts.

Everyone gasped. But try as he might, his
stepbrother had eaten too many peanuts to
squeeze into the shorts.

So Cinderboy drove away with Eddy Prince to begin a new life as Royal Palace's star player.

But being a kind sort of boy, he soon forgave his wicked stepfather and his greedy brothers and arranged for them to have as many free tickets as they wanted to see Royal Palace play.

He even offered to pay for the operation to have the glass-studded boot removed from his stepbrother's foot.

And Cinderboy lived happily ever after, and scored more goals for Royal Palace than there are peanuts under all the sofas in the whole wide world.